This book belongs to:

....

Dedication

For Tom... who always believed in me and kept my
own prickly problems in perspective... with so much love.

Fly with the angels my love...

For more information regarding permission,
please write to BiffBamBooza@gmail.com.

Biff Bam Booza and associated logos
and trademarks are trademarks and/or
registered trademarks of Waterhole Productions LLC.

Publisher's Cataloging-in-Publication data
Names: DaVeiga, Cheryl, author. | Peres, Luis Felipe, illustrator.
Title: The prickly problem / written by Cheryl DaVeiga; illustrated by Luis Peres.
Series: Biff Bam Booza
Description: Nashville, TN: Waterhole Productions, LLC, 2022. / Summary: Quirky, magic-potion-making
Dr. Pete the Porcupine finds himself in a sticky situation, perplexed by a terribly tricky case.
Identifiers: LCCN: 2022904840 / ISBN: 978-1-958050-00-2 (hardcover) / 978-1-7363951-9-6 (paperback)
/ 978-1-958050-01-9 (ebook)
Subjects: LCSH Porcupines--Juvenile fiction / Friendship--Juvenile fiction / Kindness--Juvenile fiction
/ Desert animals--Juvenile fiction / Humor fiction / BISAC JUVENILE FICTION / Animals / General /
JUVENILE FICTION / Humorous Stories / JUVENILE FICTION / Social Themes / Emotions & Feelings /
JUVENILE FICTION / Social Themes / Friendship
Classification: LCC PZ7.1.D33688 Pri 2022 / DDC [E]--dc23

Dr. Pete the Porcupine

The Prickly Problem

Written by
Cheryl DaVeiga

Illustrated by
Luis Peres

Dr. Pete the Porcupine was no ordinary doctor.

He was able to mix magic potions and use them to solve prickly problems.

And in the hot, dry desert where he lived, his neighbors had plenty of prickly problems.

Dr. Pete was able to solve every one of them - until one strange day...

Dr. Pete

It began as a typical Monday.

Dr. Pete pulled on his puffy coat so he wouldn't poke his patients.

He opened his office door and smiled at the long line of neighbors who greeted him.

"Who's first?"
Dr. Pete asked cheerfully.

Jake the Snake raised his tail.

"Dr. Pete, my rattler is not rattling," Jake groaned.

"Ahh," said Dr. Pete, as he boiled up some **Tall Tail Snake Oil** and carefully dipped Jake's tail into the soothing potion.

"That should do it!"

Dr. Pete gave Jake a hug.

"Thanks, Dr. Pete!" Jake cried as he slithered away, his tail rattling louder than ever.

Prickly problem solved!

"Who's next?" asked Dr. Pete.

Sting the Scorpion stated that his stinger stung.

Dr. Pete whipped up a batch of **Rash Bash Butter**, rubbed it on Sting's stinger, and gave him a hug.

"Wow!" exclaimed Sting. "That butter made it better!"

Prickly problem solved!

And so the day went on...

Dr. Pete smeared **Flim Flam Jam** on Rhoda the Roadrunner's sore ankle and gave her a hug.

Prickly problem solved!

Liz the Lizard's dry skin was treated with **Lizard Lotion** and a cuddle.

Prickly problem solved!

At the end of the long day, Dr. Pete hung up his puffy coat and walked out of his office.

He was surprised to see his patients waiting for him outside.

"Dr. Pete," said Jake, "we need your help.

We have a **prickly** problem
we can't solve without you."

"Oh guys," Dr. Pete said.

"I'm so tired. What is it?"

"It's Cactus Jack!" Liz cried.

"He's just **SOOOO** nasty!"

"yeah, he's mean!" Rhoda agreed.

"Very mean!" rattled Jake.

"Here's the thing," explained Sting.

"No one can pass him without hearing an insult.
He makes us feel awful."

"And we have to go past him to get to you, Dr. Pete," Liz added.

"You can solve **everything** with your potions! Please help us!"

Dr. Pete hesitated.

He knew Cactus Jack was a rude dude and this would be a hard case to crack.

"Okay, okay," Dr. Pete finally said.

"I'll go take a look."

The gang followed Dr. Pete out to the dry patch of desert where Jack lived.

Jack saw them coming.

"Well look who's here," he scoffed.

"My **prickly** problem doesn't need solving.

Sorry, DOCTOR, but I don't believe in your silly potions!"

"Oh dear! This is a **prickly** problem indeed!" proclaimed Dr. Pete as he examined Jack's skin.

"Hmm... needless to say, at least your needles are nice and sharp."

Dr. Pete mixed up some **Grouch Be Gone** potion.

Liz crept up and poured the potion into Jack's mouth.

GULP! Jack let out a belch.

"Not working, Dr. Porky Spike!" he spat.

Dr. Pete mixed up some Cranky Cure.

Then he applied **No More Mean Cream**. Nothing helped!

"Sorry guys, there's nothing more I can do here,"
Dr. Pete said, packing up his bag.

As Dr. Pete turned to leave, he felt a drop of rain on his back.

But wait... there wasn't a cloud in the blue desert sky.

Dr. Pete shined a light up at Jack's eyes.

"Jack," he asked gently, "are you crying?"

"Nonsense!" Jack replied.

"Cacti don't cry!"

But seeing the tears gave
Dr. Pete one last idea.

"I need to examine Jack's heart,"
he said to the gang.

"We can help!" cried Liz.

Rhoda ran like lightning and returned with Dr. Pete's puffy coat.

Liz and Sting crawled up between the cactus needles, dragging Dr. Pete's medical bag.

"Hop on my back," Jake cried, as he coiled his body and lifted Dr. Pete up.

"Grab onto
Jack's needles."

Dr. Pete climbed
up... up... up...
all the way to
Jack's heart.

But as Dr. Pete reached up to rub some
Heart Hurt Healing Jelly
on Jack's heart, he slipped.

Dr. Pete threw his arms around Jack, trying to hang on.

He hugged Jack with all his might.

He hugged so tight that Jack's spiky needles poked through his puffy coat. "OUCH!"

But Dr. Pete didn't let go.

And then something *magical* happened...

Jack smiled and said softly,
"Oh Dr. Pete.
I feel so much better.
Thank you, my friend."

Jack gazed down at his desert neighbors.

"I'm sorry for calling you names and hurting your feelings.

I guess it was just that I was lonely.

My heart was hurting and I took it out on you."

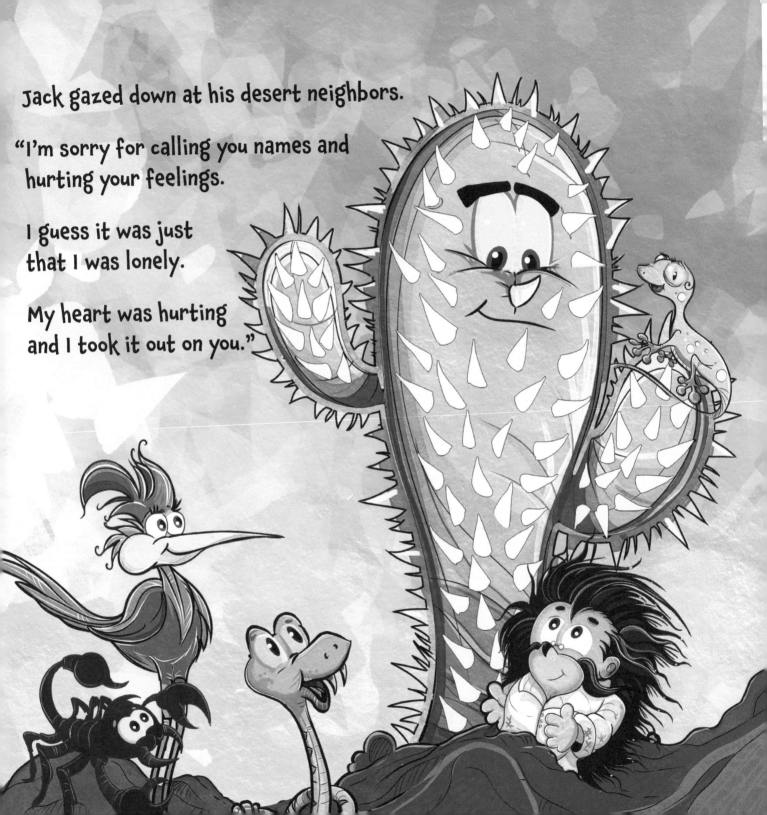

The neighbors rallied around Jack for a group hug.

"It must have been the magic potions." cried Sting.

"Of course it was!" the others chimed in.

But deep in Jack's heart, he knew the truth...
the magic wasn't in the potions.

The magic
was always
in the
HUGS!

Fun Facts About
Porcupines

- A group of porcupines is called a prickle. (Seriously!) Maybe that's why Dr. Pete is good at solving prickly problems.

- Porcupines have thousands of sharp quills on their backs for protection. That's why Dr. Pete had to wear his puffy coat to protect his friends.

- Porcupines like to come out at night, but Dr. Pete liked the daytime as well.

- Baby porcupines are called porcupettes. They are born with soft quills, but it only takes a few days for them to sharpen up. Be careful petting a porcupette!

- So, if you were out at night, a prickle of porcupettes could poke you as they passed by. Now that would be a prickly problem!

Read, Sing and Get Your Giggles On.

We hope you enjoyed this Biff Bam Booza book.

www.biffbambooza.com

Go to Biff Bam Booza.com where you can:

- Sing along to the Dr. Pete/Cactus Jack song
- Find other Biff Bam Booza books and sing-along videos
- Join the Biff Bam Booza Kids Club and get lots of goodies

It would mean the world to us
if you left a review. Scan the QR code
or visit the link.

www.bit.ly/Review-PricklyProblem

Check out these other titles!

ROCKET RED

A Little Ant with
a Big Dream

ROCKET RED

Activity Book

**WAR AT THE
ICE CREAM STORE**

Mustachio Pistachio
vs Bully Vanilli

**WAR AT THE
ICE CREAM STORE**

Activity Book

ABOUT THE AUTHOR
Cheryl DaVeiga

Cheryl DaVeiga is an award-winning songwriter who loves to combine humor, rhyme, and wordplay to create stories that bring on the giggles. She made her debut as a children's book author with *War at the Ice Cream Store*, co-written with Nashville songwriter, Dave Gibson. After receiving numerous awards, Cheryl followed with another Reader's Favorite 5-Star rated book, *Rocket Red: A Little Ant with a Big Dream*.

Each of Cheryl's books has a song to accompany it. The song for *The Prickly Problem* was a semi-finalist in the prestigious International Song Competition.

Cheryl's books and songs, videos, and sing-alongs, can be found on her site for kids: BiffBamBooza.com

ABOUT THE ILLUSTRATOR
Luis Peres

Luis Peres has been professionally illustrating dreams for thirty years. He lives in the south of Portugal and illustrates from his home studio by the ocean. In addition to children's books, Luis has illustrated children's history books, and has created art for video games, apps, animated series, board games, posters, prints, logos, and greeting cards. His preferred artistic style is imaginary worlds, fantasy themes, and science fiction environments.

Luis works for both traditional publishers and independent authors. You can learn more about Luis on his site: icreateworlds.com

CPSIA information can be obtained
at www.ICGtesting.com
Printed in the USA
BVHW022047290722
643394BV00001B/1